LUKE MANGAN

Reindeer
Flight School

To order additional copies of this book, contact:
Xlibris
844-714-8691
www.Xlibris.com
Orders@Xlibris.com

ISBN: 978-1-6698-2030-7 (sc)
ISBN: 978-1-6698-2029-1 (e)

Print information available on the last page

Rev. date: 04/19/2022

Reindeer

Flight School

It's Christmas Eve, kids need to get to bed soon. Because Santa Claus is on is way here. Emily said, but wait. Tell us, Grandpa.

How did Santa get his flying reindeer?

Well, you know that. He wanted to deliver presents to children around the world. Flying in his magic sleigh.

So Santa had animal try-outs to pull his sleigh, and many kinds of animals came.

Like a kangaroo from Australia, he said sorry, kangaroo, your hopping would make for a bumpy ride. The elephant from Africa was shivering and realized he did not like cold weather. When he was standing in the long line, waiting to see Santa. He said I hope that I do not get sick. I know how that goes with my nose.

But the buffalo said I like cold weather! I'm from Yellowstone, I'm a bison, just saying. Santa said, but you weigh over a ton, and you are too rough and tumble. You can't easily land on a rooftop softly.

Santa saw the reindeer in the woods nearby.
He thought that they would be best. I'll
have to train them to run fast to be strong
and have graceful landing skills.

So Santa asked the reindeer if they would like to
try-out to pull his sleigh, and many reindeer came.

He chooses Sargent elf to train the reindeer.
So he started the Reindeer Flight School.

The reindeer lived in the barns next to Santa's castle.

On the other side of the castle was the elves' workshops where they made the toys. In the back of the castle was the Christmas Tree Forrest.

The reindeer are fed magic feed to make them fly. Magic feed is made of peppermint, gingerbread, and chocolate. The magic of Christmas makes them joyful. So they take leaps of joy to start flying.

The reindeer ran around the race track to see which were the fastest. The reindeer practiced every day for months. They practiced running games and skill of jumping off and landing on rooftops. They pulled heavy load on sleds and their built strength. Reindeer had to have the courage to fly. Self-confident to land on rooftops.

They had to stay committed to their practices and training every day. Then on graduation day, it was time for the big race. That they would swiftly fly around the North Pole. Then the eight best reindeer were chosen by Santa.

Then when Christmas Eve Night came. Santa teamed up his reindeer on his magic sleigh, and they flew all around the world, delivering presents to all the good boys and girls. They flew supersonic speed over the oceans in just a minute. Santa and his reindeer have continued every year since. Merry Christmas!